FAITHFUL

WHISKEY RUN

HOPE FORD

Faithful © 2021 by Hope Ford

Editor: Kasi Alexander

Cover Design: Cormar Covers

MILLIE

WHAT DID I EVER SEE IN HIM? I ASK MYSELF AS I stare through my office window out into the store. Mike Miller, my ex-boyfriend, keeps making faces at me through the window as if we're still friends or something. But we're not. I'm definitely not stupid enough to put myself in that position. Well, not twice anyway. I learned my lesson the first time.

Mike comes to stand in my doorway and stares at me with a big smirk on his face. "What you doing, Millie Moo?"

I cringe at the nickname. At one time, I thought it was sweet, the way he always seemed to say it with affection as he would wrap his arms around me. But now, not so much. Not since I discovered that he was only dating me to get the manager's position at my father's store and the fact that Millie

Moo wasn't really a term of endearment. He was making fun of my plus size figure.

The Whiskey Run Farmer's Co-op is owned by my father. I'm the office manager, and my dad has been looking for a store manager for some time now. He's wanted to retire for a while, and there's no doubt the man deserves it. He raised me pretty much on his own since my mother left town when I was young. His whole life has been me, our ranch, and the co-op. Now he wants to spend more time on his ranch, and there's no way I'm going to mess that up for him. I can put up with an ex-boyfriend if it means my dad gets a break.

"What do you want, Mike?" I ask him, unable to keep the disgust out of my voice. I've really tried to be nice to him since everything happened, but to say it's hard is an understatement. If my dad knew what kind of man Mike is – a two timing, using cheater – there's no way he would have promoted him. But I'm between a rock and a hard place, and I chose the option that seemed like it would be better for my dad, even though I've second-guessed myself a thousand times since making the decision.

"I was thinking that if you ever decide you want something scratched – I'll take one for the team – I'll scratch your itch." He finishes his asinine statement with a wiggle of his eyebrows, and I roll my eyes at him. Thank God I never slept with him. If I had I probably never would have forgiven myself.

Luckily, I figured out exactly what kind of man he was before I gave in.

"That's never going to happen, Mike, so like I've told you before, if you don't have anything to talk to me about work, then don't talk to me at all."

I spin my chair away from him and act as if I'm digging for something in the file cabinet. I've learned the best way to get rid of Mike is to ignore him. He can't stand that.

I keep digging, and when I don't hear him anymore, I assume he's given up and walked away. That is until I hear a soft knock on my door. Already fed up and frustrated, I bark out, "What Mike? What do you want?" as I turn to face the door.

With my mouth hanging open, my dad looks at me with a grim look on his face. "Hey, honey."

"Hey, Dad," I say and bolt up from my chair. I've done my best to hide my true feelings about Mike from my dad, but too many more outbursts like that one, he's not going to believe it.

"Millie," he starts, and I hold my hands up because I know exactly where this conversation is going.

"Dad, it's fine. I promise. Mike and I are fine."

He's shaking his head and walks farther into my office. "I know it has to be hard to work with an ex-boyfriend. All you have to do is say the word and he's gone."

I stare back at him, and it's on the very tip of my tongue to admit what truly happened with Mike and me. There's no doubt if my dad knew the truth, Mike would be gone. But just as I'm about to say it, I remember everything my dad has sacrificed for me, and my lips slam shut while I shake my head side to side.

"Millie, there's something you're not telling me. I know it. I know you." He stresses the *you*, and bile starts to rise in my throat. I hate lying to my dad. The guilt is too much.

"Dad, it's fine. I promise. Now, why did you come in to see me? Did you need something?"

He shakes his head. "No, I was just going to go down to Red's and pick up lunch. I wanted to see if you wanted anything."

I lean over and pull open my desk drawer and heft my purse out. "I'll go. I need to stretch my legs after sitting at this computer all morning. What do you want? Your usual?"

If my dad notices me hustling past him, walking backwards to the door, trying to get away from all his direct questions, he doesn't say anything. "Yeah, my usual."

I put a smile on my face. "All right. I'll be right back."

I push through the front door of the co-op and get a block away from the store before I slow my pace. Lying to my dad is definitely taking its toll. I walk another block and take deep breaths to try and calm myself. First, dealing with Mike and then having to deal with the lies to my dad are enough to wreak havoc on a person.

I stop outside Red's Diner and peek in. I see Violet, one of my best friends and the owner of the diner, standing behind the counter. I pull my shoulders back and push through the door. When the bell above the door chimes, Violet looks up with a smile pasted to her face, no doubt about to greet a newcomer. When she sees me and the look I thought I had hidden well, she shakes her head. "What's wrong?"

I look around the restaurant as I stride up to the counter. Red's Diner is the most popular place to eat in town. It's the hangout of all hangouts. It's where all the gossip seems to start, and with Violet yelling across the restaurant at me, asking me what's wrong – well, I'll be the first name mentioned tonight on the chatterbox as everyone forms their own opinions of what is wrong with me.

"Really? Did you have to scream that across the restaurant?"

"Sorry. I saw the look. You know the one. It's the *I've been dealing with my dumbass ex-boyfriend because I want to be some kind of martyr so my dad can retire* look."

I take a seat at the counter and am thankful that even though all the tables and booths seem to be occupied, the stools at the counter are still open. "Violet, we've been over this."

She rolls her eyes. "So did you come for a lecture from your best friend or are you wanting to place an order?"

"I'm getting lunch for Dad and me."

"Your dad want the usual?"

I give her the *What else would he order?* look. He's been ordering the meatloaf and mashed potatoes ever since Violet added it to the menu. It's definitely his favorite.

"What about you, Millie? Hamburger today?"

Just the thought of eating one of the diner hamburgers makes my mouth water. But I started a diet this morning. Another one. I shake my head. "No, I'll take the Cobb salad with grilled chicken. Lite ranch dressing on the side."

"Millie..."

"It's what I want, Violet. I don't need the speech today." She's my best friend, and she knows how sensitive I am about my weight, but I still shut her down. No doubt she's going to tell me how pretty I am, and I don't need to lose weight. It's the same thing she's always saying to me. But obviously if what she says was true, I wouldn't have the nickname "Millie Moo" from Mike.

Violet shrugs her shoulders and then points to the dessert case next to her. "Okay, you want to eat rabbit food for lunch. Have at it. But are you sure you don't want a slice of your favorite apple cinnamon Blaze cake?"

She's pointing at the spongy goodness with the cream cheese frosting, and if it was any other day, I would give in. The apple cinnamon Blaze cake is my favorite. Its key ingredient is the cinnamon whiskey that is made at the distillery at the edge of town. It's what our town, Whiskey Run, is named after. But I take a deep breath and blow it out, telling myself to be strong. "No, no cake for me today."

Violet puts both hands on the counter and leans toward me. "You don't need to be on a diet, Millie."

I point toward Eddie, who's standing at the cooktop. "You going to put my order in? I have to get back to work."

Violet flings her hands up in the air, shaking her head. Honestly, if I let her loose, she'd give Mike a piece of her mind. I have no doubt about it. She's the one that was there for me when I found out that Mike was sleeping with another woman and was only dating me to get the manager's job. Probably the worst of it was hearing him tell someone on the phone that there's no way he would ever sleep with me because he's afraid I'd smother him while we were in bed. I can't stop the grimace on my face, and I look around the restaurant as if the people here could hear the thoughts in my head.

Luckily, no one seems to even notice me. At

least no one seems to. That is until I look to my left, at the far end of the counter away from everyone, where a lone man is sitting. He's rugged looking with at least a couple days of stubble on his chin. He has longer hair and the most piercing blue eyes I've ever seen. He's staring at me, and instantly I can feel my whole body heat. A million things cross my mind. Did he hear me say I was on a diet? I look up at the ceiling, deep in thought – did I say anything about Mike and what happened with him? Geez, I hope not. I definitely don't need someone else speculating on what they think happened. I have enough of that going around already.

Because I can't stop myself, I chance another look at the stranger. At closer look, I notice that he's older. Considerably older than my twenty-four years of age. He has to be in his late thirties. The corner of his lips raise in a smile, and he nods his head in acknowledgement. Normally, I'm a nice person. I'll say hi to anyone. But I guess not today, because I barely stop my mouth from dropping open. The hot guy smiles at me. I turn my back to him. It's rude and uncalled for, but I don't know what else to do. I'm not good at small talk, and there's nothing good that can come from me talking to the hot cowboy. It's obvious he's way out of my league. And he's obviously not from around here. I definitely would have remembered him. I gaze out at the restaurant, but no matter how much I focus on the locals, waving and calling hello across the restaurant, I can still feel the hot, penetrating gaze of the man behind me. I look through the big window that shows Eddie, the cook, and I can see that Violet is bagging up my order. Thank goodness. I need to get out of here. It definitely feels like the temperature has gone up a notch – or thirty.

"All right, here you go. A meatloaf and a Cobb salad with grilled chicken, blah, blah, blah."

I can't help but laugh out loud as I hand over the money. "Vi, I'm sure that's not how you're supposed to describe your food to customers."

She rings up the order in the register and makes change with the money I gave her. She hands over the change. "I'm only saying that because I hate the way that stupid Mike has made you feel about your-self. He's an idiot."

I nod my head quickly and don't dare look over at the stranger. No doubt he's hanging on our every word. "I know, Vi. I've got to go. Thank you for lunch." And because she's my best friend and means well, I tell her, "And thanks for the pep talk. I love you, friend."

Now, Violet is the one that's trying to get away. She hates any kind of affection and does anything to avoid it. She pulls the towel from the belt at her waist and flicks it at me. "Go. Get outta here. Enjoy your salad. Talk to you later."

I give her one last wave and walk out the door. I

tell myself I'm not going to look inside but of course, I don't listen. I look. I about have to strain my eyes to look through the reflection on the glass to see inside. But there he sits. Completely turned around in his stool, watching me as I walk down the sidewalk. And all I can think is, *Don't trip, Millie. Don't you dare fall on your face.* I lift my shoulders back and keep walking. The guy may be hot, but I definitely don't need a man in my life. Not now.

Austin

IMAGINE MY LUCK. I never come into Whiskey Run. My ranch is right on the border of Whiskey Run and Jasper. The farmers co-op in Jasper is closer, and that is my main reason for ever going into the town. So the fact that not only did I have the best lunch I'd had in a long time, I saw the prettiest, curviest, brown haired woman I'd ever seen. Already, the day is looking up.

I watch as she walks down the sidewalk until she's out of eyesight. I hated to let her go without even asking her name, but the way she turned her back to me, she definitely didn't seem interested. And then hearing her and the waitress talk about some guy named Mike breaking her heart pretty much sealed the deal for me. She doesn't need or want a man hitting on her. So I let her go. But I'm a big believer in fate. If it's meant to be, our paths will cross again.

Even knowing all that, I still can't resist asking the waitress about her. "So, uh Millie... the woman you were talking to..." I start, hoping that she'll get to talking without me having to actually ask the question.

But instead the waitress with the nametag that says Violet crosses her arms over her chest. She seems like she's ready to defend her friend, and already I can tell I'm going to like this woman just for the fact that she seems like a good friend to Millie. "What about her?"

"Is she seeing anyone?"

She looks me up and down and then puts her hand on her hip. "Who wants to know? I don't know you, and I know everyone in this town."

"I'm Austin Yates. I own the Yates ranch at the edge of town."

"You mean the big one as soon as you get into Jasper?"

I laugh. "Actually, the majority of my land is in Whiskey Run. I just don't spend a lot of time in town since Jasper is closer."

"Well, if you prefer Jasper then what are you doing here?"

I almost laugh at her question, but I can tell she's being serious. I never answer to anyone. Most people take one look at me and don't question me. This woman is definitely protective of her friend. "I'm in town to meet with Mr. Ogle at the Whiskey Run Co-op to talk about setting up an account."

Violet smiles and looks me up and down. I definitely feel like I'm being judged. She crosses her arms over her chest with a smirk. "Millie works at the co-op. Her father, Rusty Ogle, owns it."

She's looking at me as if she's trying to gauge my reaction, as if I have some sort of plan or something. Maybe she thought I already knew about Millie and her dad. But I can't stop the slow smile that forms on my lips. If that's not fate, I don't know what is.

"Be nice to her," she threatens as she hands me my ticket and tells me the total I owe for my lunch.

I unroll a twenty from my money clip. "You never did answer my question. Is Millie seeing anyone?"

"You'll have to ask her that."

I point to the dessert case. "Fair enough. I'll take a piece of the cake too."

"Which one? Chocolate? Or the apple cinnamon Blaze?"

"The apple," I tell her as I set the money on the counter in front of me.

She boxes up a slice of cake and sets it in front of me before picking up the money. "Got a sweet tooth? You can't go wrong with the apple cinnamon Blaze."

I just shake my head. "It's not for me."

She gets my change out of the register and hands it to me. "Is that for Millie?" she asks, gesturing to the Styrofoam carton between us.

"Yep. She looked like she wanted it."

She puts her hands on the edge of the counter. "Well, Mr. Austin Yates, there may be some hope for you yet then."

I thank her for my meal and walk out of the diner with a light step. Even though I feel like I got the third degree, I at least feel like I may just have a chance with the curvy Millie Ogle. There's no way her protective friend would give me the go ahead if not. I pick up my pace, excited to find out and see Millie again.

2

MILLIE

I KNOCK ON MY DAD'S DOOR TO HIS OFFICE AND walk in to set his food on his desk. "Here ya go. Meatloaf and mashed potatoes."

He claps his hands and rubs them together. "Thanks, sweetie. My favorite."

"You're welcome. You going back to the ranch after you eat?"

"No, actually I have an appointment. Then I'll be heading home."

"All right, Dad, but you know the whole point of you hiring Mike as the store manager was so you could spend more time at home."

He opens the package of food and inhales deeply. "I know. I'm going as soon as my meeting's over."

"Okay, love you."

"Love you too. Thanks for the food, honey."

I walk back to my office, completely avoiding Mike, and take a seat at my desk. I pick through my salad and wish I had just gotten the cake instead of what I ordered.

"I'm here to see Millie."

The voice is one I don't recognize, and I slide my chair a little to the side so I can see out the opened door into the store. I almost choke on a piece of lettuce when I recognize the hot cowboy I just saw minutes ago at the diner.

Mike moves and blocks my view. I can hear him talking. "I'm the manager here. Anything you need or have a question about should be directed to me."

I roll my eyes and stand up, wiping my already sweaty palms down the front of my pants. I walk toward the door. "I'm Millie. How can I help you?" I ask the stranger.

He smiles when he notices me and bypasses Mike without another glance. "Hey, can we talk for a minute?"

"Uh, sure, come on in." I gesture to the seat in front of my desk and walk around to the other side. I need to put some distance—and my desk— between us. My mind is going a million miles a minute, wondering what he wants with me.

"I'm Austin, Austin Yates. I saw you at Red's."

I know I'm blushing, and I know it's not pretty. Some people blush, and it brings out their complexion and makes them even prettier. I'm not that kind of woman. I blush and it looks like I just ran five miles and overexerted myself. "Yeah, I saw you." I stutter the words and clear my throat, hoping he doesn't notice how he's affecting me. Obviously I was wrong. I need more than a desk between us because even now the room feels ten degrees hotter.

He opens the bag he's carrying and sets a small carton in front of me. "Well, I brought you this."

With a lump in my throat, I ask, "You brought this for me?"

"Yeah, I wanted you to have it."

I almost giggle, but I hold it in. This man with the handsome face, kind eyes and big smile brought me something. But just as soon as my excitement starts to rise, my delight fades in an instant. "Why?"

He shakes his head as if he's confused by the question. I mean, it's understandable. I don't know this man. Why would he bring me something? "Yeah, why would you bring me something? You don't know me."

He scoots the chair up to the desk and leans his elbows on it. "Maybe because I want to get to know you."

I don't know what to say to that. I'm not the girl that most people flirt with. Actually, I have zero experience with flirting. So instead of answering him, I open the carton, and my stomach drops. It's the apple cinnamon Blaze cake. The one that Violet and I were talking about. The one where I told her I couldn't eat it because I was on a diet. My weight has always been an issue, and there's no doubt the man heard the whole conversation.

I close the box and try to give him my best smile. "Thank you."

He shakes his head. "I thought you liked that kind of cake."

"I do. Thank you, really. I appreciate it." I see Mike's head as he keeps popping up in my doorway and the window, no doubt wondering what the man wants with me that he couldn't help him with. He looks as if he's biting at the bit to get in here.

I'm about to get up and show Austin to the door when he interrupts me. "I know this is awkward, but this is me. I don't know any other way to be. I saw you at Red's. I think you're pretty and man, if you bring out the protective side of Violet like you do, you have to be a good person. I want to get to know you. Would you have dinner with me?"

I almost laugh because I can just imagine the conversation he had to have with Violet in order to get any information about me. But even though he's handsome, I can't just go out with a stranger. "I normally don't go out with men I just met."

His eyes darken. "That's good. I wouldn't want you to." He looks almost possessive, as if the thought of me going out with someone else bothers him. I don't have time to dwell on it before he continues. "So what do you want to know about me? I own the Yates ranch, it's out on the edge of town right before you get to Jasper. It's been in my family for fifty years. I have a camp in the summer to help inner city teens. I donate to the children's wing of the hospital in Jasper. I'm kind to animals." His smile deepens as he stares into my eyes. "And I just found out today that I'm a sucker for a woman with long black hair, brown eyes, and a pretty smile."

My mouth falls open. It's on the very tip of my tongue to say yes. Gosh, whatever he wants I would give in this moment. He's definitely charming. But something stops me. "So what are you doing in Whiskey Run today?"

"I'm here to meet with your dad, Rusty. I actually am late for our appointment, but I had to stop and see you first."

As soon as he says my dad's name, I freeze. The smile stiffens on my face, my arms lock on my chest, and I'm pretty sure a corner of my heart just froze over too. "Wait, you have an appointment with my dad? That's why you're here?"

This time I do get up. I put my chair in front of me trying to put even more distance between us and squeeze the back of it. Of course I'm not going out with him. He's just another man—another Mike— that thinks dating me is going to get him something from my dad. I should have known that the handsome man that shows up out of the blue wouldn't be interested in me. That doesn't happen in my world.

He stands up too and holds his hands out. "I'm here to see you, but yes, I have a meeting with your dad also."

I roll my eyes. "Well, I'm sorry, I don't date men that are doing business with my dad."

He brings his hands together in front of him and nods. "Fine, I won't do business with your dad."

I gasp. Surely, he's joking. I mean, I just met the man, but surely he's just saying that. I walk to the office door quickly and out of it. Austin follows me. It was either that or he was going to be left alone in my office. I walk quickly to the back of the store where my dad's office is. I don't even have to turn to know that Austin is on my heels. It's like I can feel his gaze on my ass the whole way. I stop before I get to the door, not wanting my dad to overhear. "Look, I won't be the reason my dad loses a client. But I'm also not going to go out with you. I just went through a breakup, and I'm not ready to start dating. So... my dad's been waiting for you. I think he plans on getting home soon, so you can see yourself in." I point to the door and walk away. Without stopping, I look over my shoulder. "Thanks again for the cake."

I stride back to my office, hoping that Austin

goes through with the meeting. Yeah, I definitely would have liked to get to know him better, but not now. And I have a perfect reminder of why not as Mike follows me back to my office. "What is Austin Yates doing here? Did you not tell him I'm the manager of the store and he should be talking to me?"

I stop and block him from entering my office. "He has a meeting with my dad, the owner of the store. Now don't you have something to do?" I tell him right before I slam the door in his face.

I take a seat at my desk and stare at the container of cake. Opening a drawer, I shove it in there and then put my head in my hands. Geez, is this day almost over or what?

Austin

WELL, that didn't go as planned. I'm not used to being turned down. I'm not being arrogant about it, but normally I have women asking me out instead of me asking them, so the fact that Millie flat-out told me no is a little surprising.

And honestly, I thought she was interested. At least until I mentioned her dad. There's obviously something going on there. I watch as she walks back to her office just as that manager Mike walks beside her. I don't like him, and I definitely don't like how he walks so close to Millie.

I take a deep breath. I'm already late for my meeting, and I know that's not making a very good impression. The fact that I want the man to like me surprises me a little. I normally don't care about shit or niceties like that. People can take me or leave me. But I know why I care. I'm going to need him on my side I think if I want to get close to his daughter.

I walk to the closed door and knock. A mere second goes by, and I hear him say, "Come in."

He's sitting in a chair with an almost empty plate of food in front of him. "Hello, Mr. Ogle. I'm Austin Yates. I'm sorry I'm late."

He waves me off. "No worries. I just finished my lunch. Have a seat. You can call me Rusty. I'm curious why you wanted to set up this meeting today."

I take a seat and look at the big man behind the desk. The only similarities between him and his daughter is the color of his hair and shape of his eyes. I clear my throat and try to focus on the business at hand.

"You can call me Austin. As I mentioned on the phone, I own the Yates ranch."

"Yeah, I know the one. It's out at the edge of Whiskey Run."

I nod. "That's right. And I've always done my

business at the Jasper Farmers Co-op. I would like to set up an account here."

He shakes his head. "Jasper must be doing something wrong. You're the third ranch this week to move their accounts here."

I shrug, not wanting to dis the company. They've changed owners, and the service and product quality has gone way down, but I don't want to get into all that. "If you have a credit app you need me to fill out, I can do that. I'll have a foreman and myself that places orders."

Rusty waves me off. "Austin, I knew everything I needed to know about you when I got off the phone with you the other day. I don't need a credit app to tell me anything. I've already learned you're honest to a fault, a hard worker and take pride in your ranch. I can't ask for more than that in a client."

I sit back in my seat. I was nervous about moving my accounts to Whiskey Run, but already I know it's the right decision. Rusty Ogle is my kind of people. "Great. I appreciate that. If it's okay, I would like to see a price list. We have some special orders we make, and I can get you that information."

Rusty nods his head. "Sure, sure. My daughter, Millie, takes care of all the ordering. She'll be able to help you."

At the mention of his daughter, it hits me then what I need to do. I just met her, but already it's important to me that I take the right step. "Actually, that's something I would like to talk to you about."

He squints in confusion.

"I mean, your daughter, sir."

"Do you know my daughter?"

I nod and shrug at the same time. "Well, I actually just met her. I brought her a piece of cake."

He sits back in his seat. "You brought her a piece of cake?"

At this point, I know I have to just put it all out there. "Yes, sir. Uh, I actually saw her at the diner. She turned down cake and she really seemed like she wanted it, so I bought a piece and brought it to her. I, uh, asked her out, sir, and she told me no."

His face has no expression. I don't know what I'm going to do if he decides not to do business with me, but I'm not even really concerned about that. I'm more concerned about the fact that he may just kick me out of here and tell Millie that I'm some kind of stalker and to stay away from me.

He finally leans forward. "Did she happen to tell you why she wouldn't go out with you?"

I move to the edge of my seat. "Yeah, she doesn't want to go out with someone that is doing business with her father or the co-op."

He throws his hands in the air. "So you gave up... chose the business instead of going out with my daughter."

I laugh then, because that can't be further than

the truth. "Actually, I told her I would take my business elsewhere then."

I wait for him to be offended, but he's not. His eyes spark at me, and I can't help but feel like I passed some kind of test. "Actually, she seemed worried about me being late for this meeting... that you needed to get home. But no, sir, I'm not giving up on your daughter. I would like to take her out."

He doesn't even hesitate. "Why? Why do you want to take out my daughter?"

My thoughts instantly go to her curvy body, how she's sexy but doesn't seem to realize it, and the excitement I saw her in her eyes when I first asked her out. But none of that I can say to her dad of all people. "She doesn't seem to smile a lot. But when she does, it about takes my breath away. I want to see if I can make her smile more."

He's quiet, as if he's weighing my words before suddenly he bangs his hands on his desk and stands up. "Right answer. Now let's go get you a date."

"Uh, sir—" I try to stop him. The thought of him playing matchmaker fills my head, and I know nothing good will come from that.

"Rusty. Call me Rusty."

I follow behind him. "Rusty, I don't think it's going to go well if you force her to go out with me."

"I'm not going to force her. She'll have the final say-so. But Austin, let me tell you this. I don't care how much business you give me. If you hurt my daughter, nothing will save you."

It's as if I can actually feel my heart palpitate at the thought of hurting Millie. "I won't hurt her, sir. You have my word."

He holds his hand out, and I know when I put my hand in his, it's not just a handshake. It's a commitment I'm making. And instead of being unsure or overwhelmed, I welcome it.

I shake his hand, and he turns again. "Follow me."

Instead of trying to stop him again, I see the smirk on his face and follow along. I sort of can't wait to see what the old man has up his sleeve.

He knocks on Millie's open door and walks in. "Millie, Austin here is with Yate's ranch. We need to get an idea of what all he needs and how much. He mentioned some special orders. I told him you would get all the information together and meet him tomorrow night to go over it all. Red's Diner okay for you. Around six?"

Millie's eyes are open wide, and she's looking between her dad and me. I force myself to look as innocent as possible, but I know she can see that something is up.

She frowns and hesitates. "Uh, we can just meet here."

I'm about to agree. It doesn't matter to me, I'll pick up dinner on the way to meet her wherever she wants to meet, but her dad interrupts. "He's working all day, honey, and he can't make it here until dinner time. But if you don't feel comfortable doing it, I can just stay late tomorrow and go over it all with him."

Rusty leans heavily against the cabinet, and I almost laugh. The man is good, and before I can even fathom that he's pulling a quick one over his daughter, I can tell she knows what he's up to. She looks at me accusingly, but I just shrug and smile. The ball is in her court, but I have a feeling she's not going to tell her dad no.

"Sure, Dad. I'll take care of it."

Rusty straightens up and puts a hand on my shoulder. "Great, thanks, Millie. C'mon, Austin, you can walk me out and you can tell me some more about what all you need." He looks at Millie. "I'll fill you in on everything in the morning."

Before he can hustle me out the door, I glance at Millie. "I'll see you tomorrow night. Be safe, honey."

Her eyes flash at the endearment, making me wish we were alone and I could just watch her face as I call her other sweet names to figure out which one she likes the best.

"Bye, Austin," she says softly.

Already, I'm looking forward to tomorrow night.

3

MILLIE

IT'S NOT TOO LATE. MY DAD MAY HAVE ALREADY left for the day, but I can still have Mike come down and meet Austin at Red's. He'd probably love it. He's pestered me all day about the Yates Ranch and if he's going to get the commission for acquiring the new business. I told him to talk to Dad.

I slow my pace as I walk down the block. My dad filled me in on some of the things Austin needs, but I'm sure he missed some of it since he didn't write any of it down. I grip the folder in my hand and swing open the door. Violet has already left for the day, and I find a booth in the corner and sit down. It's probably good Violet is not here. I was on the phone with her all of last night because she wanted the details of what happened when Austin brought me the cake. She gave me the lecture on how I shouldn't judge all men. They're not all like

Mike, she said. But luckily once she got on the subject of Mike, she couldn't stop. She really doesn't like that man. Probably as little as I do.

I order a water from the server and let her know I'm waiting on someone else. The restaurant is getting crowded with the dinner rush, which makes me cringe a little knowing that there's a possibility I'm going to be the talk of the town... again.

I go through the file in my hand, making sure I know the ins and outs of what we're going to discuss. I people watch and when I get tired of that, I pick up my phone. It's six-fifteen, and I look outside just in time to see Austin jogging up the sidewalk. He opens the door and stands there as he looks around the restaurant. He looked good yesterday, but if possible, he looks even better today. He's got his cowboy hat on and tight blue jeans on. His thighs are thick, and goodness, I couldn't take my eyes off him even if I wanted to. As soon as he spots me, his lips widen, and his white teeth look even whiter since he seems like he's covered in a film of dirt. He strides across the restaurant, and almost every head, especially the women, turn and watch him. He slides into the booth across from me, and it's then I remember that I have my mouth hanging open, and I slam it shut.

"I'm sorry I'm late. It's been one of those days."

I tilt my head to the side and really look at him.

Up close, he looks tired and worn out, but he's still smiling. "You look like you had a rough day."

"Yeah, things didn't go as planned."

"We can reschedule," I tell him. And even though I doubted going through with this meeting the whole day, I would admittedly be upset if he took me up on the offer to cancel it.

"No way. Unless you're embarrassed to be sitting across from me right now." He looks down at himself and slaps at his shirt as dust goes flying. He coughs and laughs. "Actually, I wouldn't blame you if you were."

I'm almost offended until I realize he doesn't know anything about me. "I'm not embarrassed. There is nothing embarrassing about ranching. I was raised on a ranch, and I know the work that goes into it."

He smiles and leans toward me. "That's good, sweetheart. Because I've been looking forward to this all day."

Another nickname. Honey yesterday, sweetheart today. But I still smile because just hearing it causes goosebumps on my arms. I clasp my hands together. "You were looking forward to going over numbers all day?"

He shakes his head. "No, I was looking forward to seeing you all day." He reaches into his front pocket and takes out a piece of paper. He unfolds it and hands it to me. "It's everything I need for the ranch. It has the amounts we normally pay, how much we need and how often. Can you match those prices?"

I scan the paper, and because I have a lot of the costs memorized I'm able to answer him with confidence. "These prices are higher than what we charge. We can beat those."

"Great. You have my business then."

"Just like that?"

He shrugs. "Just like that. Now we can have dinner."

"Actually," I interrupt him, "if that's all the business we have to discuss, I can go and let you..."

"No way, Millie. I came prepared so we wouldn't have to talk business. I want to get to know you."

As soon as he says it, the server appears. "Sorry about that. We're filling up fast. Have y'all decided what you want to have?"

Austin looks at me and darn it, that look he's given me is causing me to feel all kinds of things. "I'll take the Cobb salad with grilled chicken and dressing on the side. And a slice of your apple cinnamon Blaze cake."

Austin's smile gets even bigger when I order the cake, and I smile back. He orders a steak and potato before the server leaves with the promise to be back as soon as the food is ready.

"Now," Austin says and leans across the table,

"if I go wash my hands, are you going to be here when I get back?"

I nod, and he starts to scoot out of the booth. But he stops as he stands up, and I have to lift my head to look up at him. He leans in real close, and he may be dirty, but damn the man smells good. "Promise me. Promise you'll be here when I get out, sugar."

And I answer without even thinking about it. "I promise."

He looks like he wants to kiss me. It would take each of us moving our faces two inches to make it happen, and I swear I can almost imagine exactly how his lips are going to feel on mine. I hold my breath, waiting. "I want to kiss you, Millie. But our first kiss is not going to happen with half the town watching. I'll be right back."

And with that bombshell, he raises up, winks, and walks toward the back of the restaurant. A few minutes later, I remember to breathe.

***

Austin

SUGAR. So far that's the winner. That's the one that brings her smile full force and makes her eyes dilate. She liked it when I called her sugar, and I know I'm going to have to stop myself from calling her that twenty more times tonight just because I want to see her reaction.

I wash my hands quickly and go back to the booth. She's sitting right where I left her, and when I sit down, I can't resist. I lean over and pick up her hand that's resting on the table. "I'm back."

Startled, she tries to pull back, but I don't let her go. "Can I hold your hand? It was either that or I was going to sit down next to you and put my arm around you. I figure you'd be more comfortable with this."

She stops pulling, and her hand wraps around mine. Whether she realizes she did it or not, I take advantage and tighten my hold on her. "So how was your day?"

She is staring at our hands. Mine is engulfing her smaller one, and it brings out all kinds of protective thoughts inside my head. She stutters when she looks up at me. "Uh, it was fine. Busy. The store was busy."

"So, tell me about Mike, the manager. I had the feeling that he liked you. Is there something going on there?"

She starts to snort and catches herself before shaking her head. "We used to date."

I can feel my chest tighten, but I make sure not to put any more pressure on her hand. "So you must have broken it off because it was pretty obvious he still has feelings for you."

She frowns. "Actually, I did break it off with him. He was dating me to get the manager's job while he was sleeping with someone else."

Surprised and a little pissed off, I grit my teeth before asking her, "Your dad doesn't seem like the type to be okay with that."

Guilt shines on her face. "He doesn't know. My dad is wanting – no needing – to take time off. He wants to retire, and I don't want to mess that up for him. I can handle Mike."

I want to ask her more about it. Actually, I want to go to the co-op and punch this Mike in the face, but it's obvious that Millie is done talking about it. Especially when she asks me about my ranch.

The server brings our food, and I reluctantly let go of Millie's hand. I tell her about the ranch and that I'd like her to come see it sometime.

We laugh and talk, and I've never been as captivated and comfortable with a woman in my life. Maybe it's the fact that she knows all about ranching. Maybe it's the fact that with each passing minute, I want her even more. But whatever it is, I wish this night would never end.

When they bring the ticket and we've both eaten a piece of cake, I walk to the cashier holding Millie's hand. I'm just not ready to let her go yet.

I ignore the stares we get from people. I can feel Millie tense beside me, but I hope it's only because she doesn't like being the center of attention and not because she doesn't want to be seen with me. "Are you parked at the co-op?"

She looks up at me. "I am. Thank you for dinner. I had a really good time."

"Me too, sugar. Come on, I'll walk you to your car."

She tries to stop me. "No, I'm sure you're parked around back. I can walk by myself. Whiskey Run is pretty safe."

I give her hand a tug and wrap my arm around her shoulder. "I'm walking you to your car."

She's fidgeting, but I act like I don't notice. We walk in silence down the block to the back of the co-op. She points to a full-size truck. "That's mine."

"A truck? I'm liking you more and more, little Millie." She tenses beside me. "What? What's wrong?"

She pulls from my arms and smiles up at me. "There's nothing little about me."

I put my hands on her shoulders to stop her. I can't stop myself. I settle her against the side of the truck and lean into her. Our bodies are pressed together, and because I don't want to have this conversation twice, I want to make sure I have her full attention.

"I thought I would need to wait to have this discussion when you knew me a little better, but I'm just going to put it out there. You wanted that cake yesterday and didn't order it. I'm not positive, but I would guess it's because something that little shit Mike said to you or something. But here's the facts. I like you. I like everything about you. I like the way you fill out a pair of blue jeans. I like the feel of your curvy body pressed against mine." I lean farther into her so she can feel exactly how my body reacts hers being so close. "And I like the way you moan and lick your lips when you eat that apple cake. So no more worrying about your diet, or skipping treats or none of that. I like you just the way you are."

Her mouth is open in awe, and I know I surprised her. Well, it's about to be an even bigger surprise because I can't stop myself now. "I want to kiss you, Millie."

She doesn't say no. In fact, her tongue pokes out between her lips as if she can't wait for it. I lean down and wrap my hand around the back of her neck. "Tell me yes, sugar."

She says yes. It's barely a whisper, but it's a yes. I press my lips into hers, and all conscious thought leaves me. Her lips are warm and soft. The kiss goes from zero to a thousand fireworks going off in my head. When her hands slide up my chest and she grips the front of my shirt, I know without a doubt I could lose control so easily with her. Her legs part, and I move one of mine between her thighs. I lift it just a little, and when I make contact with the hot heat between her legs, she moans loudly, and I force myself to pull away with a groan. Too much more of that, and I'll have her in the cab of her truck.

"Go out with me," I demand. "Let me take you on a proper date."

She blinks and stares up at me. Her mouth is glistening, wet from the kiss we shared, and I want to run my tongue across her plump lips. She shakes her head as if she's been in a daze before finally answering me. "It's not a good idea. You're doing business with my dad."

I put my hands on each side of her face. "I'm not like Mike. I wouldn't date you to get something from your dad. And I sure as hell wouldn't cheat on you."

In that instant, she realizes she still has my shirt in her hands, and she lets go quickly. "Men are not always faithful, Austin. I know that."

"If you were mine—fuck baby, even if you aren't mine, I can't imagine looking at another woman."

She shakes her head. "What is it with you? Honey, sweetheart, sugar, baby, little Millie. You like nicknames or what?"

"I like watching your face light up when I call you a different name. So far, I think you like sugar and little Millie the best."

She laughs and tries to slap me on the chest, but I grab her hand instead and hold it tight. "Go out with me."

It's on the tip of her tongue to say no, and I take a deep breath. I don't think I can let her walk away if she says no. "Maybe," she draws out. "Let me think about it."

I kiss her quickly and pull away. "I'm not giving up on you, Millie. Now get in your truck and be safe on your way home. If I don't let you leave now, I'm going to try to talk you into all kinds of things that I don't think you're ready for."

She's about to ask me what things, and I swear if I put a voice to the things I've thought about doing to her, there's no way she's going home alone tonight. Instead of asking, though, she climbs up into her truck. "Bye, Austin. Thank you."

She puts the truck into gear and pulls out of the parking lot. I stand and watch until the lights are gone in the distance. It isn't until I get into my own truck that I realize I didn't get her number. I'll have to call the co-op tomorrow because even though I just met her, I don't want to miss even one day of talking to her.

4

MILLIE

Two days. It's been two days since my dinner with Austin, and I haven't seen hide nor hair of him. I keep waiting for him to show up or to at least call, but he doesn't.

Alan, one of the delivery drivers for the co-op, interrupts my thoughts with a knock on my open door. "Hey, boss lady! The shipment for the Yates ranch came in. You want me to deliver it before I do the others?"

At the same time, the phone on my desk starts to ring. Making a quick decision, I tell Alan, "No. This first one I'm going to take. Load it in my truck."

I wait for a questioning look or some kind of curiosity, but Alan never gives it. He just nods. "You got it." I guess it helps that I've been working at the co-op since I was young. I've done every job here and am always pitching in to help out.

The phone rings again, and I notice it's on my line instead of the store's line. "This is Millie. How can I help you?"

A shrill voice comes over the line. "Millie? Is this Millie Ogle?" the woman asks.

"Yes, this is Millie Ogle."

"Do you know an Austin Yates?"

I sit up in my chair. "Yes, I know Austin."

The woman lets out a deep sigh. "Well, thank you sweet baby Jesus, I found you. My name is Carrie."

"Uh..." I start, confused and a little unsure with where this conversation is going.

"So, yesterday morning Austin got thrown from his horse."

"Oh my God, what? Is he okay?" I'm already standing up and gathering things together before I stop myself. "Is. He. Okay?" I ask again.

"Yes, yes... he's fine. He's stubborn as a mule. Has a concussion, banged up his knee and broke a rib or two, but he'll live. That is if I don't kill him first."

I fall back in my seat. "Okay... so does he need anything?" There's a gazillion questions I want to be asking her. Like who is she? Austin made it seem like there wasn't a woman in the picture, but who is this that's calling me? Better yet, why is she calling me?

"Does he need anything?" she spits out. "Yeah, he's going to need a new housekeeper if he keeps running his mouth like he is. Look, he was in the hospital, and it seems he didn't have a phone, and apparently I'm going to lose my job if I don't call you. You work for a family for twenty years and you'd think you'd get a little respect. He just wanted you to know why he hasn't called you. But I'm calling you for help. His foreman—heck, all the cowboys are going to walk out of here unless someone can calm him down. He's been a bear."

"Okay. And you think I can calm him? You do know I just met him a couple days ago."

"Honey, it's worth a shot. I've never seen him so upset, wanting to make sure you weren't mad at him. I swear he would've called himself, but I'm pretty sure his vision's still blurry even if he won't admit it. He's going to do permanent damage to that hard head of his if he doesn't listen to what the doctors are telling him."

"Okay, I'm coming. I mean, I'll give it a shot. I have his order too, so I'll bring that with me."

"Okay. I'll see you soon. Thanks, Millie. I'm gonna owe you one."

And before I can say anything else, she's already hung up.

I grab my purse from the desk drawer and

walk out the back of the store to my truck. Everything's already loaded, and I holler thanks to Alan before getting in and pulling out. I go by my house first. It's a little two-bedroom house that sits on the edge of my dad's ranch. I pack just a few things and then jump into the truck and head toward Jasper and the Yates Ranch. I'm crazy. This is probably the craziest thing I've ever done. It's almost a thirty-minute drive, and I try to take that time to plan what I'm going to do, but instead all I can think about is that kiss we shared the other night.

When I pull in to the long driveway, I slow down to take it all in. My father's ranch is nice. It's small and well maintained. But this place is something else. There are multiple huge buildings, including a huge two-story house with a big wraparound porch. The view from here is magnificent. It's almost like you can reach out and touch the Jasper Mountains.

Seeing the way he lives just makes me realize exactly how different we are. I make a decision, right then and there, that I'm going to drop off the order, make sure Austin's okay, and get the heck back to my side of town.

A few cowboys spot me pulling in, and I recognize Austin immediately. I barely get stopped next to the huge metal barn before he breaks away from the group. He's limping, holding his side. His hat is down low on his face, and he's squinting. No doubt the afternoon sun is hurting his head.

I take a deep breath and open the door and jump down from my seat. Holding my hand up to shade my eyes, I look at him smiling back at me. "Hey, Austin. I heard you had a run-in with a horse."

He waves his hand. "I'm fine. Better now that you're here."

"I have your order. Let me know where you want it, and I'll unload it."

"Carter!" he hollers and instantly winces. Even yelling is hurting his head. "Can you unload this?" he asks the man as he comes walking up to us.

"Sure thing, boss," the man named Carter says as he stops beside us. "So you must be Millie?"

I look between Austin and the man named Carter, a little surprised that he knows my name. "I am. I'm from the Whiskey Run Farmers Co-Op." I hold my hand out to him, and I swear I hear Austin growl. He must really be hurting. Carter squeezes my hand and smiles at me.

"And she's taken," Austin snarls.

My eyes snap to Austin, and a tremble shoots down my back. His heated glance is trained on me, and my nipples harden at the rough sound of his voice. "I, uh..."

Carter laughs. "Trust me. I could have guessed that for how much you talked about her today." He rolls his eyes and walks to the bed of my truck. "I hope since you're here you can get him inside where he's supposed to be."

"Really, Carter. This is my ranch. It's my name on the gate at the end of the driveway... I'm pretty sure if I want to stand outside on my ranch I can do it."

Obviously, Austin is not a good patient. I point to the load in my truck. "Carter, do you want my help unloading..."

"You're not unloading shit. I'll be damned if I'm going to have my woman unload my order..."

The way he says "my woman" sends a little thrill through me, but his words still agitate me. I cock my hip out and put my hand on it. "I'll have you know that I can do anything a man can. As a matter of fact, I can usually do it better." I turn to Carter. "No offense, Carter."

CARTER HOLLERS from the back of my truck, "None taken."

When I turn back around, Austin is standing toe to toe with me. He puts one hand on my cheek and the other one at my waist. "I have no doubt about that. The fact is, I don't want you to. Not when you've got me right here to share the load."

"Austin, you're hurting. You hide it well, but I can see it on your face. You can't be lifting things.

As a matter of fact, I'm pretty sure you're supposed to be resting your ribs and sitting in a dark room for your concussion."

Carter walks by with a load in his hands. "Good luck with that. I've tried all morning to get him inside."

I shake my head. I had a clear plan in my head. I was going to be in and out. But now I can see that I may really be needed here. He's obviously not taking care of himself. Austin's hand moves around my back and pulls me in. His cheek is resting against the top of my head, and I swear I hear him sniffing. "Are you smelling me?"

I can feel his cheek move into a smile. "Yeah, and you smell good. A cross between sunshine and honeysuckles."

Man, how can I have only met this man a few days ago and already he's got me so turned upside down I can't stand it? "So I have an idea."

"I'll do it," he says without hesitation.

I pull back enough to look up at him. "You don't even know what it is."

"Fine. If it involves me and you, possibly sitting in a dark room, then I'm in."

He's smiling, but I can see the pain on his face. He's tried his best to hide it. I pat him on the chest. "Fine, let's go." I reach for his hand and thread our fingers together and give him a little tug.

He falls into step beside me. "So do I get to pick what we do in the dark room?"

I laugh out loud. "Don't hold your breath there, stud."

He wraps his arm around my shoulder, and we're both smiling as we walk up the steps to his house.

Austin

"OH GOOD HEAVENS, HE'S SMILING." Carrie, my housekeeper, says as we walk in the front door. Carrie's been with my family for what seems like forever. She's more like family than anything. I thought for sure she'd leave me when my parents passed away, but she didn't. She stayed right here with me.

"Har, har," I say before turning to Millie. "Honey, this is Carrie. She takes care of the house and me half the time."

Carrie tucks a few gray strands of hair behind her ear. "Yep, so now I won't have to quit, it seems. Your girl's here now, so I'm hoping you're going to be a little nicer to be around." Her smile deepens as she looks at Millie, and I can tell she already likes her. "All I can say is good luck."

Millie laughs, and I can already tell that these

two are going to be thick as thieves together. "I haven't been that bad."

"Ha!" Carrie spits out and starts laughing. "I love you like a son, and I quit my job five times today. Yes, you've been that bad."

I shake my head. It's all a joke, but honestly I don't know what I'd do without Carrie. "You wouldn't ever leave me. You love me."

"I just said I did," she deadpans with an eyeroll at Millie. "That concussion's got him messed up more than he's letting on. I'm going to go back to my room for the night. I know Millie came straight from work, so I've left you some dinner on the counter. Just call me if you need anything."

"Thanks, Carrie," Millie says to the retreating woman.

"Sure thing, honey. I'm hoping to see more of you."

Millie blushes when she looks at me, as if she's trying to gauge my reaction to Carrie putting us together. The fact is, I'm hoping for the same thing. I want Millie around. More than I should probably admit for only knowing her a short time. "I'm glad you're here."

"So what do you think? We eat, then find a television somewhere in this big house and maybe turn the lights down real low —"

"And you'll let me hold you while we pretend to

watch television." Even I can hear the hope in my voice.

She lifts her shoulders in defeat. "Sure. If it will get you to rest, I'm game."

Because I can't resist a minute longer, I kiss her. It's a brief kiss. One that reminds me of exactly how explosive we can be together. I pull away and show her to the kitchen. Picking up the plates, I ask her to grab two drinks out of the refrigerator.

"What do you want?" she asks.

"I'm good with water."

She grabs two waters. "Me too."

"Follow me." I lead her into the living room, and she gasps behind me. No doubt because of the room. I get this reaction a lot.

"This is your living room?"

I set the plates on the coffee table and grab a remote that lifts the top up to the perfect height to eat from. "Yep. Have a seat."

She's looking all around the room, her mouth hanging open. "This is, wow, this is amazing."

I try to look at it from her perspective. The floor is carpeted in a thick ivory beige, which Carrie hates. She has to have the cleaners come at least once a month to clean it. The furniture is big, dark chocolate wood. The couch is huge and takes up most of the room. The wall hangings are ones that I had specially painted of my favorite spots on my ranch. But probably the centerpiece of the whole room is the big screen television hanging from the ceiling. I spared no expense on this room because it's where I am most of the time when I'm home. "Thanks, sugar. I'm glad you like it."

She sits down on the couch and starts to fidget. "Austin, what am I doing here?"

I sit down next to her and wrap my hand around her knee. "I was sort of hoping you're here because you wanted to be here."

"I do. I mean, I wanted to make sure you were all right. I should go."

I laugh and put my hands on her waist when she tries to get up. She falls back to the couch in a huff. "This is crazy. I don't belong here."

"I say you do." I give her one of my charming smiles, but she's still stubbed up and looking uncomfortable.

"Look, I'm going crazy here. My doctor says to rest, and I'm willing to do that since you're here with me. We'll eat. We'll watch some TV. We'll get to know each other."

I try to adjust how I'm sitting and wince as I feel my ribs catch. I suck in a deep breath of air and try to readjust. "Are you okay?" she asks worriedly.

"Yeah. I'm fine," I tell her with bated breath. I try to smile, but I know it's only a grimace that appears on my face.

The only saving grace for being in pain is the fact that it looks like I might get some sympathy from Millie. She grabs my plate off the coffee table and holds it out to me. "Here you go. Eat."

I take the plate, and she picks up the remote and turns the television on. "What do you want to watch?"

"I don't care," I tell her, staring at her from the side. I want to reach out and push the hair behind her ear. I want her eyes on me, but I know I need to work up to it.

She laughs. "I've never known a man not to care what's on TV. As a matter of fact, I'm surprised you even let me hold the remote."

I'm torn. I want to ask her about the other men in her life but just the same, I don't want to know either. "Things like that don't matter to me. Plus, I'd rather watch you than the television."

She jerks her head toward me, and the surprise that lights up her face is evident. She's blushing, and in this moment, I know she's the prettiest woman I've ever seen. "Get your food and eat."

She grabs her plate, and instead of eating on the coffee table, she sits back and holds it in her lap. We're right next to each other. I can feel the warmth of her thigh pressed against my leg, and a calm comes over me. The last few days have been filled with stress, from blurry vision, headaches, my ribs and knee, I've been a downright asshole. But now that she's here, it's like everything is right in the world.

She eats slowly while I scarf down the sandwich, chips, and apple slices. When I'm done, I set the plate on the table and lean back with my water. She seems self-conscious, so I try to act like I'm watching television instead of completely aware of everything she's doing.

When she finishes, she stands up and grabs our plates. "No, it's fine. Leave them."

She walks a few steps. "Give me just a few minutes, and I'll be right back."

She isn't gone long, and when she comes back she sits at the far end of the couch. I laugh.

"What's so funny?"

"You. Really, you think putting space between us is going to stop what's happening between us?"

She lifts her chin. "I don't know what you mean."

I slide across the cushions and trap her into the arm of the couch. "Yes, you do. For whatever reason, you're questioning all of this. Why I want you here. If you should trust me. And well, I'm glad you're asking those questions because just the fact that you're wondering about them tells me that there's hope for me. I'm not going to let you down, sugar."

She rolls her eyes. "There's that name again."

I put my finger under her chin and bring her head up. "You like it. You know you do."

Her gaze holds such intensity, it's almost

vibrating off her. "I do like it, Austin. I like it when you call me sugar, honey, baby, all of it. But I don't want to be hurt by you, and even though we just met, I know you could destroy me."

"But I'm not going to."

She looks as if she may argue with me, but she stops. "Forget it."

"No, obviously this is something we need to talk about."

She nods. "Yeah, we probably should. But not now. Not when you feel the way you do. Let's just sit here and enjoy the movie and rest."

I put my arm around her shoulder and bring her into my side. Luckily, she doesn't stiffen. She melts against me, and I lean my chin against her head. We watch television for I don't know how long before I can feel my eyes getting really heavy. With her heat against me, I fall into the best sleep I've had in a long time.

5

MILLIE

I FELL ASLEEP. IT'S MORNING, BUT THE SUN HASN'T come up yet. I'm tucked against Austin, his arm around my waist as we lie with my back to his front. I can feel the steady rhythm of his breathing all around me, and I bask in the safety I feel in his arms. It would be way too easy to get used to this.

I slide from his arms and onto the floor. On my knees, I look at him. Me getting up didn't even faze him. He's still sleeping. I look at the soft expression on his face, and I'm glad to see that he was able to sleep so well.

I tiptoe out of the room. Luckily, I have some things in the truck, so I go and grab them and freshen up. When I come out of the bathroom, Carrie is in the kitchen. She's cooking breakfast, and I debate on whether I should leave or not. "I got a late start this morning. Breakfast will be ready in a little while."

"Oh, I think I'm going to head out—"

But before I can even finish, she points the spatula she's holding at me. "Don't think you can just leave while he's sleeping, honey. Knowing him, he'd just drive into town and follow you, and he's not supposed to be driving for a week."

"Okay, do you think he'd mind if I walked around the ranch? It's so beautiful, I'd love to see it at sunrise."

"He wouldn't mind. Just stick close to the barn."

I nod and head out the front door. There's already a number of people out, and it looks like they are feeding the animals. I walk around, taking in the horses whinnying, the talking and laughter of the men as they work, and the hay being thrown from the hay loft. I take a deep breath, and the smell of dust, dirt, and horse hide fills the air around me. I couldn't stop the smile that overcomes me if I wanted to. My family's ranch and this one may be very different, but the feel and smells are the same.

I walk over to the corral and see the lone horse trotting around. She whinnies every now and then. I cluck my tongue, and the horse freezes. She holds steady and very slowly swings her head toward me. She twists and turns her head before slowly walking toward me. When she gets close enough to the fence, I climb up and sit on the edge with my hand held out. She breathes in my scent and moves closer, rubbing her head along my jean-clad thigh. I walk down the side of the fence and land in the dirt with my hand still on her velvet hide.

Running my hand along her mane, I ask her, "How are you doing, pretty girl? Why are you out here by yourself?"

I hear an intake of breath behind me, and I turn, expecting to see Austin but instead, Carter the foreman is standing there staring at me with his mouth hanging open.

The horse instantly starts to back up, and I start cooing to her to settle her. With one hand on her bridle, I stroke her nose with the other, all the time talking to her in a low encouraging voice.

"Well, I'll be damned."

"What was that, Carter?"

"Uh, sorry, ma'am. It's just no one on the ranch has been able to do anything with her since Austin saved her from the slaughterhouse. Each day we get a little step closer, but she about bit the man that put the bridle on her this morning. She's the one that threw Austin, too."

"What? But you're so sweet," I tell the horse, instead of answering Carter.

He snorts behind me.

"Can I ride her?"

"I don't think that's a good idea. Austin probably wouldn't be happy about it."

I look at him pleadingly. "Carter, I was raised on a ranch. I know about horses, and this one wants to go on a run. Just around the corral."

"She won't let you saddle her."

If that wasn't a challenge I've never heard one. I spot a saddle hanging over the fence and go to grab it. I approach the beautiful white horse, and she stands completely still as I saddle her and doesn't even seem upset when I tighten the belt around her stomach. "You're a good girl, aren't you?" I look at Carter. "What's her name?"

"I don't think the boss has named her yet. We were waiting for her to name herself. Ornery comes to mind."

"Bite your tongue. I'm thinking Patches. She looks like a Patches to me." She's white with brown fur in patches down her back.

I grab the reins and pull myself up on the horse. She tussles around, but doesn't seem to object to me sitting astride her. I give her a small kick with my heel and cluck my tongue, and she starts to move. I start off slow, but it doesn't seem either of us is happy with that. We take a few turns in the corral before I let her loose. We gallop around, and even though I have almost all the cowboys standing at the fence, all of them staring in amazement, I'm laughing and happy. It seems I've made a new friend.

Austin

I WAKE UP, and before I get too far off the couch, Carrie lets me know that Millie is outside at the barn. I rub my hands across my face and go upstairs to shower real fast and go outside to find her. There are flutters in my stomach just at the thought of seeing her again. I woke up a few times in the night, and every time we had our arms wrapped around each other. Now, in the light of the day, I have all kinds of thoughts in my head. I'm attracted to Millie. I was the first time I saw her, and even though I knew I wanted to date her, I know I won't just settle for a date or two. The way she is, her kind heart and loving way about her makes me start to imagine all kinds of things. The fact that she came when she knew I was hurt and stayed the night with me tells me that she likes me and gives me a little hope.

As soon as I step off the porch, I notice there's a gathering at the corral. It seems everyone is goofing off this morning instead of working. That is until I spot Millie on the back of the unruly horse that threw me yesterday. I have to fight the urge to run toward her and save her. The only thing that stops me is the big smile on her face. Her long black hair is blowing in the wind, and she seems happy and at home. She's something else up there, and I'm not the only one that is noticing. All my men are smiling at her; it's as if her carefree happy attitude is drawing them all in. I could stand here and watch her all morning, but worry fills me. No one has been able to do anything with this horse. I don't even know how this happened.

I get to the fence, next to my foreman. "Carter, what is she doing out there?"

"Boss, she obviously knows her way around horses. Look at her."

"I am looking. You need to quit looking." I address the rest of the men. "All of you need to quit looking – get to work."

They all give me a smirk. I know what it looks like. I've just met the woman and already I'm going crazy over her, but I don't care. I want to be the one that looks at her.

She spots me, and her whole face transforms. She looks worried and rides over toward me. "You're supposed to be resting."

I hear the snickers of the men walking away, and obviously she does too.

She blushes prettily. "I mean, since you're not feeling well, you should be in bed."

It's killing me to have her up on the back of the

wild horse, but I don't want to make any sudden moves. The closer she gets to me, the more skittish the horse seems to get. "I'm more worried about you. That horse..."

"Is the sweetest horse I've ever met." She slides down, and only when her feet hit the dirt am I able to breathe easier. She grabs the lead and walks, petting the horse's mane. "From what Carter said, I'm thinking she had a male owner, and he wasn't very nice. I mean, he made it sound like Patches doesn't like men, but what do I know? I mean, there could be women on this ranch all the time."

She won't look at me. I know what she's asking without actually asking me. "Honey, there's not any women that come here. Carrie stays in the house or in the garden, but she doesn't ever come down to the barn. You're the only woman that's been here in a very, very long time."

She smiles but tries to stop herself by biting her lip. Clearing her throat, she shrugs. "Well, then maybe my theory is right."

"So, Patches, huh?"

She starts to stutter. "I mean, that's just what I called her when I was talking to her. I'm not trying to name your horse or anything. You should pick out her name."

I take a step closer to her, real slow like. When Patches doesn't seem to mind, I take another step. "Sounds to me like she's your horse now."

"I can't take your horse."

I reach up and brush the hair off her face. "She's yours. But you'll have to come here and see her."

She puts her hand on her hip. "You don't just give people horses, Austin."

"I'm not giving people a horse. I'm giving my girlfriend a horse."

"Girlfriend?"

I lean in and nuzzle my mouth right next to her ear. "Girlfriend." I can't resist, so I kiss the lobe of her ear, and she gasps. My shaft hardens in my jeans, but all the pain in the world is going to be worth it for this curvy woman that has already turned my world upside down.

"Let's get Patches settled, then we'll get some breakfast."

She leans up on her tiptoes and kisses me on the lips. I don't react because this is the first time she's reached for me, and I don't want to scare her. I know I have the goofiest smile on my face. "What was that for?"

Her eyes are clouded in desire, and I'm doing my best not to stare at her erect nipples pressing against her shirt. With a thickness to her voice, she says, "I just wanted to kiss my boyfriend. Is that all right?"

"Baby, you can kiss me any time you want."

6

MILLIE

A WEEK. IT'S BEEN A WEEK SINCE I RODE PATCHES that morning and Austin called me his girlfriend. He's called and texted me every day, sometimes just sending me pictures from his ranch and a lot of times pictures of Patches.

He hasn't been able to drive, so he's had one of his hands bring him into town, and we've had lunch at the diner a few times or just walked around town holding hands. It's already all over Whiskey Run, and people are asking me about my new boyfriend. Normally, I hate being the center of attention, but Austin has brought out the confidence in me, and I smile and introduce him around town.

My dad and Austin have hit it off. Probably because they have the ranches in common. They can talk for hours about auctions, the price of feed going up, and all the other things you face on a ranch.

I keep waiting for Austin to try and take our relationship to the next level. But besides the several kisses, he's been a complete and utter gentleman. Which, to be honest, is a little worrisome. I'm ready to take our relationship to the next level, but there's no way I can tell him that. I'm definitely going to have to let him take the lead.

This morning he was cleared from the doctor, so he asked me out to dinner to celebrate. There's no way I was going to say no. I've found myself more and more excited to spend as much time as possible with him.

We've grown closer with all the time we're spending together, and the fact that we call and text throughout the day has helped me get more comfortable with the idea that maybe not all men are unfaithful. Because I've watched Austin. When we're out, he only has eyes for me. All of his attention is focused on me. I've never been around a man as affectionate and attentive as him.

Lost in thought, I'm staring at my computer screen, knowing I have more work to do, but I can barely concentrate knowing Austin should be here any time.

A knock on my open door brings a smile to my face. I'm of course expecting Austin, but it's Alan.

"Hey, boss. Can you come and look at a shipment real quick?"

I stand up and follow behind him. "Sure thing." In passing, I see Mike and ask him to let Austin know I'll be right back if he shows up.

Mike just grunts at me. If anyone has had a problem with my relationship with Austin, it's been Mike. He's made sure in every way possible to bring me down and to try and make me feel insecure. I've forced myself to ignore him. I'm not worried about what Mike thinks about anything.

Austin

I'm crazy about her. She's all I want. The only thing I think about anymore. I'm walking into the co-op and bypass Mike to go straight to Millie's office. When I see she's not there, I turn to Mike. "Hey, you seen Millie?"

"Yeah, she had to go out back for a minute. She said she'll be right back."

I nod, debating whether to go find her or wait. I hate spending any time with Mike, so I'm about to start walking when he stops me.

"You and Millie dating?"

Automatically, my hands fist at my sides. I hate

to even hear her name on his lips. "Yeah, we're dating."

The smirk on the other man's face pisses me off. And as soon as he starts to talk, I want to punch him in the face. "She doesn't put out. I mean, not that I mind or anything, I still got the job, but –"

He doesn't get another word out. He's struggling for breath because I have him pushed up against the counter with my hand around his neck. He's pulling at my arm, but I'm not letting go. "I don't want you talking to her, about her—hell, I don't want you looking at her. You got that, you son of a bitch?"

"That's hard to do since I have to see her fat ass all day."

I lift my knee and hit him in the nuts. When he doubles over, I punch him in the face, and he falls backwards, holding his dick in one hand and his nose in the other. "Enough. You want me to kill you or fire you? I'll let you pick."

"You can't fire me," he says as he spits blood out on the floor.

I barely restrain from kicking him in the face with my boot as I walk by him. "Watch me, motherfucker."

I'm panting when I get to Rusty's door, and there's fire raging through my veins. I still may have to fight the guy even after he's fired.

"Hey Austin. How's it going?" Rusty says as I stand in the doorway.

"Austin. What's wrong?" Millie comes up behind me, and her touch on my back instantly soothes me, reassuring me that I've done the right thing. She's so sweet, so beautiful, I'm not going to let anyone talk about her the way Mike did. Ever.

"Tell your dad about Mike, Millie. You tell him, I tell him, or I go out there and kick the shit out of him some more. It's your choice."

"It's not your place..." she starts.

I'm surprised by how gentle I am when I wrap my hand around the base of her neck. "It's my place. I'm making it my place. I'm not going to stand by and let him or anyone else talk about you like he was. It ends now, Millie."

She obviously can see how upset I am. She wants to do what she thinks is right for her dad, but it's not going to happen like this. She turns to him, and it's my turn to comfort her. I thread our fingers together. "Dad, uh, Mike only dated me because he wanted the manager job. He was cheating on me."

"Why didn't you tell me?" Rusty asks, stunned.

"Because you deserve time off. You've been planning to retire for so long, and it was finally going to happen, and I didn't want to mess that up for you."

Rusty comes around his desk and stops in front of his daughter. "Millie, you're the only thing that matters to me. Not this store, not the ranch we live on, nothing." He shakes his head, no doubt disgusted with himself that he hired a man that disrespected his daughter. "I'll take care of it."

"But Dad..." Millie starts, with guilt in her voice.

I cut in, because I'm not going to stand by and let her talk him out of it. "Rusty, I have a hand that is way overqualified for his position. He's trustworthy, a hard worker, and has a family. Can I send him in"—I hold my hands up in front of me—"on a trial basis. If he doesn't work out, you fire him, and I'll take him back out to the ranch. I just want to help."

Rusty rubs his beard. "What do you think, Millie?"

She leans back into my warmth. "Dad, if Austin says he's good, then I believe him."

Rusty agrees with her. "All right, have him come in tomorrow."

"Sir, we're going to dinner, but I can stick around and help out with Mike if you want before I go," I offer. A part of me is hoping he wants my help because I'd like to get in another lick or two. Another part of me is ready to get Millie out of here and away from the asshole.

I'm not surprised when Rusty turns down my offer. "Thanks, but I can handle Mike."

Millie hugs her dad bye, and I walk with her

hand in hand to the front to grab her purse out of her office. As we're walking out, she has a tight grip on my hand. We pass Mike, and she holds me even tighter. I give her a quick smile before turning to Mike. "Rusty needs to see you."

Mike, with blood on his shirt and still wiping at his nose, frowns at us. But as soon as we get out the door, I ask Millie, "We have reservations at the Peddler. You want to walk there or drive?"

With her eyes lit up, she says, "It's going to be a nice night. Let's just walk."

I tuck her under my arm. "You're right, sugar. It's going to be a nice night."

7

MILLIE

He's so calm. I saw the blood on Mike's shirt. I know he and Austin must have fought, but Austin is completely composed and seemingly unruffled. Not me, though. I'm a case. I'm actually freaking out a little. We sit down to eat at Peddler. The décor is farmhouse with big country style tables, and they have the best steaks in Whiskey Run and Jasper combined.

"What are you having?" Austin asks as we sit down at the table.

I shrug, looking at the menu. I know exactly what I'm getting, but I feel like if I look up at him he's going to know exactly what I'm thinking right now.

The server walks up to the table, and before she can get the whole phrase out of asking what we want to drink, I interrupt her. "Can I get a shot of the Blaze Cinnamon Whiskey and a water?"

"Sure, are you ready to order?"

"Yes. Steak, medium well and side salad."

"Sir, what can I get you?"

Austin is staring at me as he orders. "I'll take a water and filet, medium with a baked potato."

Austin takes my menu and stacks it with his before handing it to the server, who retreats from the table.

As soon as the server walks away, he asks me, "Are you okay?"

I nervously giggle. "Yeah, why wouldn't I be?" What I want to say is *I've never had a man stick up for me like you did*, but I don't. I keep that tidbit to myself.

Luckily, he doesn't ask again, because the server brings back our drinks.

"Did you know that the Cinnamon Blaze Whiskey is the number one selling whiskey from the Whiskey Run Distillery? That's what Violet uses to make her apple cake too. It's very popular."

I lift the small glass to my lips, and the cinnamon burns my nose as I inhale the hot scent.

I watch him as he picks up his water glass. I look between our two drinks. "Should I not be drinking?"

He shakes his head. "You can drink whatever

you want. I won't let anything happen to you or take advantage of you, if that's what you're worried about."

I am just about to put my lips on the drink when I stop suddenly. "So if I drink this, you won't take me home with you tonight?"

My face heats, but I don't care. I know I was going to wait for him to make the first move, but I'm done waiting.

His eyes darken. "Do you want to come home with me tonight?"

I nod, and he takes a deep breath. "One drink. I want you sober later."

My whole body trembles at the promise I hear in his words.

***

Austin

SITTING through the meal is pure torture. She can't drop a bombshell like that and then not expect me to lose my mind. I hustle her through the meal, but she doesn't seem to mind. Neither one of us can keep our eyes off the other, and damn if it isn't the most sensual foreplay I've ever been a part of.

We're walking back to the co-op, and she's holding on to my arm. Her skirt is swishing around her legs as she walks, and I can barely refrain from touching her right here in the middle of town. We talk about the ranch and how well Patches is doing with people now.

"I can't believe you tried to give me that horse, Austin."

My voice is husky and thick. "I'd give you a dozen horses if I thought it meant you'd spend more time with me."

When we get to the parking lot, she starts to walk to her truck, but I stop her. "Uh, uh, sugar. You're riding with me."

"But I have to work in the morning, and I'm sure you do too."

But I'm already pulling her to my truck and opening the passenger door. "It doesn't matter. You're going with me. I'll bring you into town tomorrow."

She doesn't argue. She pulls herself into my truck, and as soon as she's seated, I shut the door and jog around to the driver's side.

I give myself a pep talk. *Take your time, Austin. You have all night. Don't rush her. Don't fuck this up.*

I pull onto the road to home and reach over to wrap my hand around her thigh. It's like her soft skin is vibrating under my palm. She's holding on to my arm, and I hate to give her an out, but I know I have to. "Are you sure about this, honey?"

"Am I sure I want you?" she asks softly in the dark cab of my truck. She's usually shy and insecure but seems to have done an about-face. I nod my head and swallow.

She doesn't answer, and I start to get nervous. We're on the two-lane out of town, and I sneak a peek at her. I finally start to breathe again when I see that nod. "Yeah, Austin, I'm sure I want you."

I pull the truck off the side of the road to a screeching halt. Gravel is flying everywhere, and I put the truck into park. I'm breathing hard, like I've been running a race instead of sitting easily in an air-conditioned truck.

"Austin! What's wrong?" she asks in alarm. She's looking out the windows in front of us and to the back.

I lift the console between us and flip it back. I lean into her, and she comes to me without question. "One taste, baby. I need something to hold me over until we get home."

I clasp my lips to her and taste her. She tastes like forever and a little bit of cinnamon Blaze Whiskey. I nip at her lip, and when she whimpers I try to pull away, but she grabs the front of my shirt and holds me where she wants me.

"Austin," she moans. She grabs on to my hand, and while she's looking into my eyes, she brings it between her legs. Her skirt has ridden up, baring her thighs to me. When she widens her legs, she's holding my arm as if she's afraid I'm going to pull it away, but there's no chance of that. Her panties are soaked, and I slide my finger into the side of her leg and stroke her hot core. Her head falls backward on a moan. "Does that hurt, baby?"

She nods. "I hurt so bad. It's like I'm wound tight and I just, uh, I don't know."

Her hips lift, urging me deeper, and I coat my fingers in her soft, wet, channel. Stroking her clit, I circle it, gauging the perfect pressure by the tiny whimpers and moans that escape her mouth. When her nails dig into my arm, I know she's close. Back and forth, around in circles I stroke the bundle of nerves. "Come for me, sugar. I want you to come."

Her legs kick out, her one hand goes to the dashboard, and her whole body clenches. I don't stop, because I want her full release. I want to give her what she needs. She continues to writhe against my hand, and when she drops back into the seat, I pull my hand away and bring it to my lips. She tastes just like she smells: of sunshine and honeysuckle.

I move to get back fully in my seat, and she's leaning toward me, her hand reaching for my leg. Her touch is feather light as she moves from my knee and up. I stop her and move our hands to the seat between us. I won't be able to get us home in one piece if she's touching me. "I need to get you home, Millie."

She scoots toward me and leans her head on my shoulder. I put the truck into gear, and she sits with her warm, soft body pressed against me the whole way. It's the longest and most frustrating ride I've ever had to make.

8

MILLIE

I SHOULD FEEL LIKE A HUSSY, BUT I DON'T. I BITE MY lip the rest of the way to his ranch. I'm squirming in my seat while his hand strokes across my leg. He won't let me touch him, and I'm going crazy. I wish I'd had some more of the Blaze Whiskey because getting undressed in front of him is going to be tough. I look at his profile and he's so handsome he takes my breath away.

When we get to his house, he comes around to help me down from the truck, but I've already jumped out to meet him. He takes my hand and pulls me through the house. I'm secretly hoping that we don't see Carrie because I know that would be embarrassing. Looking at the two of us, there's no doubt what we're about to do.

We walk up the stairs and into his bedroom.

He barely gets the door shut and he's pulling at my shirt. "I can't wait. I need you now."

When he starts to pull my shirt up, I catch his hand in mine.

"Millie." He cups my jaw. "I don't want to rush you. No matter how much I want this, I'll wait until you're ready."

"I just..." I start and stutter to a stop.

"What is it? You can tell me anything."

He walks me over to the bed and sits on the edge, patting the space beside him. I sit awkwardly next to him, my back straight, looking anywhere but at him.

"I'm not like the other woman you've dated."

The smile slides onto his face easily. "I know you're not. You're not like anyone I've ever known."

I scoot closer to him and slide my hands up his chest and wrap them around his neck. I want him so badly, and even though this is embarrassing, I need to say it. "I'm fine with who I am. I like me."

"I like you too, Millie, and so help me if you're about to tell me you don't want me to see your body or something crazy like that, I'm going to lose it, because right now, I'd probably sell the ranch to see you right now."

I lean in and kiss him. He tries to deepen the kiss, but I pull back. "I wasn't going to say anything about my body, I figure you already have an idea of what you're getting there, but thank you for that. I won't make you give up the ranch; this is going to happen."

His nostrils flare, and he looks into my eyes. "Then what is it?"

"I'm not really that experienced, and well, I just don't want to disappoint you, that's all."

His hands tighten on my shoulders. "Millie, what are you saying? Are you a virgin?"

I blink at him, trying to keep the embarrassment off my face. "I, uh, no; there was one time when I was eighteen."

"Fuck," he swears. He pulls me against his chest, and I can feel his heart pounding under my ear. "Baby, I don't want to hear about another man with you."

I shake my head. "No, I just thought you should know. I may need you to tell me when I'm doing something wrong. I just don't want to disappoint you."

He grabs my hand and presses it to the large bulge between his legs. "Does it feel like there's any way you could disappoint me? Just looking at you makes me feel things I've never felt before."

The sincerity I find in his gaze has me standing up. I kick off my shoes and pull my skirt down my legs. When I stand up, I reach for the hem of my shirt, take a deep breath, and lift it over my head. I wore my matching black panties and bra set today, and the way his gaze traces over my body, I know I made the right decision.

"Finish," he says with a thick voice. "I want to see all of you."

My body trembles at his command. I reach behind me and unsnap my bra and let it fall to my feet. My breasts, large and heavy, sway with my heaving chest. I pull my underwear down my hips and let them fall, kicking them away. When I'm completely naked, I stand up, pull my shoulders back, and look him straight in the eye. There's a huge part of me that wants to cover myself, and I can't help but wonder what he's thinking as he looks at my rounded body. But I'm not going to let those thoughts ruin this for me.

"It's your turn," I tell him.

He grabs me around the waist and pulls me so that I'm standing between his legs. My hands go to his shoulders to steady myself. "Let me look at you," he says as his hands slide up my ribcage. He cups my breasts in his hands and kneads them.

I grip his shoulders tighter. "Austin," I moan as he pulls my nipple into his mouth. He sucks, sending a tremor through my body. I can feel the desire between my legs as his mouth and hands caress me everywhere.

He moves up my chest, putting open-mouthed kisses along my shoulders and neck. He stands up and fits his lips over mine. Before I know it, I'm lying down on the bed with him standing over me.

He undresses quickly, and I can't take my eyes off him. There's a smattering of hair across his chest, and my first thought is I want to feel it across my cheek. He's muscled and defined, and just looking at him causes a pull in my lower belly.

He climbs onto the bed, and I widen my legs so he can fit between them. His hard length is against my thigh as he reaches between us and strokes his finger through my swollen, needy folds as a low groan leaves his lips.

My orgasm from earlier still has me extra sensitive to his touch. "Austin..." I moan as I lift my hips to meet his hand.

Austin

She's a seductress and doesn't even know it. The way she stripped confidently in front of me had me chomping at the bit to get my mouth and hands on her. She's moving her hips against my hand, wanting another release, and I can't wait to give it to her.

"I need to be inside you, Millie. I need to feel you come."

Her moans deepen, and she reaches for me,

pulling me by the forearms until we're face to face. "I want that too."

I let my forehead fall to hers. "I'm clean."

Her eyes widen. "Me too. And I'm on the pill."

I don't wait to examine why her being on the pill bothers me. That's something I'll have to think about when I actually have blood running to my brain because right now, it's all running south.

She reaches between us and wraps her hand around my length. I hiss on contact and pull my hips. I don't want to come in her hand like some teenage boy. "Fuck, baby, you have no idea what you do to me."

She smiles and strokes me again from root to tip. "I have an idea."

I position myself and line up at her core. She widens her legs, and I push slowly inside her. I have to take it slow, or I'll come in an instant. Her pussy is tight, and already with only my tip in has me in a vise.

"You okay?" she asks as I realize I'm holding completely still. Her smile is lethal as her vaginal walls tighten even further on me.

There's no other choice. I push in, sliding into her honeyed depths, and this time, she's moaning with me. We move our bodies in tune to each other. Her pussy is drenched, and I pick up the pace, loving the way she feels as if she's made just for me.

Her eyes are on me, wide and aroused. My most

genuine smile stretches across my face. How did I get so lucky to have this woman in my bed?

I reach between us and stroke my finger through her folds before pleasuring her clit. She starts to writhe underneath me, and our thrusts become manic. The only sound in the room is our breathing and the sounds of our bodies slapping together.

"Yes, Austin. Right there. Please don't stop."

With her urging, I give her all I have. In and out. Thrust after thrust, I make her mine.

When there's no more holding back, I tell her to come, and her body thrusts one more time before she tautens, overcome by the orgasm coursing through her body. She's held so tightly, I grunt as I move in and out of her, releasing my cum deep into her sex.

I hold myself over top her and kiss her.

I lie to the side and pull her against me, never breaking our kiss. She molds her body into mine.

When I pull away, she surprises me. "Can we do that again?"

I laugh, a deep one that comes from my belly. "Yeah, sugar. We're going to be doing that a lot."

I pull from her arms. "I'll be right back."

I'm gone only a minute before I'm back beside her with a warm washcloth. I clean her up and then clean myself up in the bathroom. When I lie down next to her, she's boneless and can barely hold her eyes open. I pull her into my arms. "Rest, honey."

I can feel her head nod on my chest, but she doesn't say a word. "You're mine, Millie."

She doesn't move, making me believe she's already asleep. I go to sleep with my arms around Millie as I try to figure out how I can keep her.

9

MILLIE

I CAN'T STOP SMILING. NO MATTER HOW HARD I TRY, I can't stop. It's crazy because I know I probably look like a crazy person. Every time my dad sees me, he makes some kind of joke about me smiling so much and then just shakes his head, asks me why I'm smiling and keeps walking. It's obvious to everyone why I'm smiling... it's because of one Austin Yates. He has completely flipped, turned me upside down. He calls and texts me every day, and he insists that he see me every day. It seems that everything is moving so fast, but also so slow at the same time. A part of me wonders if this is really my life. How did I end up with the hot cowboy?

I'm standing at the front of the store. I just went over a few things with Ranger, the ranch hand that Austin sent to try out the manager's position. He's been a godsend. He's already helped so much with the store, my dad has been able to spend more and more time at home on the ranch.

My phone dings in my pocket, and already smiling, I know it's probably Austin. I open the texting app.

Change of plans for tonight.

That's all it says. I don't text him back right away because I'm waiting for him to say something else. When a few minutes go by, I text him back. *Ok.*

I get back to work, and even though I'm wondering what's going on, I know he'll text or call me before I get off work.

Hours go by, and when it's time for me to head home, I grab my purse, look at my phone one more time, tell Ranger I'm leaving, and walk out the front of the store. I get to the edge of the parking lot and freeze. Austin is standing next to his truck with his arms wrapped around a woman. Pain squeezes my heart. I swear I'd never believe it if I didn't see it with my own two eyes. I turn quickly and run back into the store. I wipe at the tears that I didn't even realize were falling. Ranger is busy putting things on a shelf, and I dash into my office. I drop my purse on top of my desk and pace back and forth. I'll wait just a few minutes and leave. What's he even doing here? All the thoughts are running through my head when the bells over the front door of the store ring. I completely stop breathing. I don't even have to look to know who it is. It's Austin... and that woman.

I walk out of the office and do my best to keep my expression guarded. But I must not be hiding my emotions very well, because Austin takes one look at me and frowns. As soon as he's close enough, he pulls me into him. "Josie, this is my girlfriend, Millie. Honey, this is my sister, Josie."

"Your sister?" I squeak out. He's mentioned his sister, but she lives in Texas. He never mentioned that she was coming into town. My stomach unbinds with relief, and I can't even try to hide it. "It's so nice to meet you." Even I can hear the relief in my voice.

Josie and I talk, and the whole time, Austin is looking closely at me.

We talk about going to dinner, and it's then I realize this must be the change of plans.

"Josie, Ranger's right over there. Why don't you go say hi and then we'll go to dinner."

Josie turns to me. "You're joining us for dinner, right?"

"Yes, she's coming."

Josie slaps her brother's arm. "She doesn't need you bossing her around, bub."

I laugh, already liking his sister. "Yeah, I'm coming."

As soon as Josie walks away, Austin grabs my

hand and walks with me to my office. He closes the door and turns me so I'm leaned up against it.

Austin

"WHAT WAS THAT?" I ask her. I knew the minute I saw her exactly what she was thinking. If I was anywhere else, I'd take her over my knee right now.

She lifts her chin. "What was what?"

I thread my hand through her hair and hold on to the nape of her neck. "What were you thinking when I walked in with my sister?"

She looks back at me stubbornly. "You don't want to know what I was thinking."

"Yes, I do."

She tries to pull from my arms, but I'm stronger, and she doesn't get far. I edge my leg between hers and cage her in between my arms. "No, let's get this out in the open so we can put it behind us."

"Fine. I saw you hugging your sister in the parking lot. I thought, well, you were together."

Well, fuck. "Obviously, I'm doing something wrong here."

She shakes her head. "No, this is not on you. This is all me. I'm the one with all the insecurities. I know what kind of man you are, and I should never had let my head go that way."

Her voice is so sad, I know she regrets it. I swear if that Mike was still in town, I'd whoop his ass again.

I bring her over to the couch and sit down, pulling her into my lap. When she's completely settled with my arms around her, I look into her eyes.

"Millie, I love you."

It's the first time I've said the words, but I mean them. I've probably loved her since the day she came to the ranch when I was hurt. "I only want you, sugar. I can't even imagine looking at another woman. It's you. You're the one. I promise that I will always be faithful to you. Nothing will ever come between us."

"You love me?"

I laugh. "Yes."

"I love you too, Austin. So much."

I lean in and seal my lips to hers. My sister will just have to wait.

EPILOGUE

VIOLET

STANDING AT THE COUNTER OF MY DINER, I LOOK around with pride. Besides how busy the restaurant is, I've actually made quite a difference in some of the patrons' lives. I've never seen Millie so happy, and I've known her almost her whole life. She's still young and deserves happiness more than anyone I know. She's having dinner with Austin and his sister, and I could watch them all night. The protective way that Austin looks at her is stuff that dreams are made of. I don't know if I'm the reason that Austin and Millie met and got together, but I like to think so. If I hadn't told him she worked there would he have stopped and talked to her that day or bypassed her office, not even knowing she was there? I like to think I've done something to help make my friend happy.

"Excuse me, are you Violet Jennings?"

A young woman walked up to the counter while I was daydreaming. She's timid and obviously shy. Her clothes are clean, but she looks so frail, I instantly want to fix her something to eat. She has a large bag over her shoulder and it looks like it weighs more than she does. "Yeah, I'm Violet."

"Hi. I'm Heather Bates. I went to the Sugar Glaze Bakery to apply for a job, but they weren't hiring. They suggested I come here."

It's on the tip of my tongue to tell her I'm not hiring, but something stops me. "Well, Heather, it's nice to meet you. Have a seat. What can I get you to eat?"

She looks taken back. "Oh, I'm not going to eat."

From the look on her face, I know exactly why she's not going to eat. I've seen it before. There have been many people come through Whiskey Run, and if they don't have any ties here, then they're here because they're running from something. I've never seen Heather before, so all I can assume is she's definitely running.

"I'll be running around, and it will actually make me feel less guilty during our talk if you are eating than just sitting here waiting on me. What about a burger and fries?" I don't wait for her to answer, instead I ask her, "You want everything on it?"

She looks like a deer caught in the headlights. "Uh, no onion."

"I got it. And a milkshake too? You like strawberry?"

She nods, and I walk away to put her order in. I'm talking to Eddie and watching the restaurant. Heather is looking around, and I see her gaze stop on something a few feet away. I follow her gaze and see she's looking at Brett Barrett. At that exact instant, Brett looks at the counter and sees Heather. For just a second, I can see the chemistry sizzle between them, but just as quickly it fades when Heather whips her chair around and puts her head down as she picks at the napkin in front of her.

I join her again and am wiping down the counter as we talk. "So what are you doing in Whiskey Run?"

There's fear in her eyes. "I'm looking for some-where... to live. I needed to move, and I ended up here."

"What kind of experience do you have?"

She shakes her head. "Not any. I wasn't allowed... I never had a job before, but I'm a fast learner and a hard worker."

Brett gets up from his booth, and there's no doubt he's heard our conversation by the way he's looking at the small woman in front of me.

He hands me his check card. "How you doing tonight, Brett?"

"Good," he grunts, and when he does, the woman jerks and wraps her arms around her middle.

Brett and I both notice it, and Brett's face turns hard. That's one thing about Brett Barrett: he's a good man. He doesn't talk to a bunch of people, but it's mostly because he doesn't trust them. He's been sort of clammed up since his fiancée left him standing at the altar.

"Hey, Brett. Are you still hiring for a house-keeper and a cook out at the ranch?"

He shakes his head, but his eyes tell me he knows where I'm going with this. "I never was hiring."

His negative response doesn't even faze me. "Well, I can just imagine how long it's been since it's been cleaned."

"I clean it," he says, not even offended.

"You're a rancher. You don't have time for that. Well, Heather here is new in town and she needs a job. Unfortunately, I don't have any openings, but I talked to her, and I think she would be perfect for what you're needing."

He's about to argue when Heather jumps up. "I can't... I can't go to his ranch."

Brett stares at her, and he takes a few breaths before he says anything. "What's wrong with my ranch?"

I hide my smirk. I was expecting him to walk

away, but obviously he's bothered by what's going on with Heather, and he's not going to leave her in a lurch.

The woman blushes prettily. "Nothing. I'm sure it's a fine ranch."

Brett snorts. "It's not. It's falling down around me. But you'd have food and shelter. You would just have to cook for me and two other guys. Maybe clean a little bit. I won't be able to pay you a lot, but you'll get room and board too. And you'll be safe. No one will bother you out there."

Heather was shaking her head, ready to say no the whole time Brett was talking, until he said the word *safe*. It's then she stopped shaking her head.

"But I don't know you," she half whispers.

"I can vouch for him. He's sort of grumpy, but he's a good guy. He wouldn't hurt a fly."

She seems to be weighing her options. She pulls her shoulders back and lifts her chin. "I don't know how else to say it, but I have to ask. Do you drink and have you ever hit a woman?"

Brett jerks back as if she slapped him. His face is covered in horror. "Fuck no. I'd never raise my hand to a woman, and I'd never let it happen around me either. I promise if you come work for me, you won't have to worry about that. And yea, I drink, but not very often. And I don't get drunk."

Eddie walks up beside me and hands me the burger in a to-go box and milkshake in a Styrofoam cup. I hand them both to Heather. "Here you go, honey. Have Brett bring you to come see me the next time he's in town."

She looks at the food in her hands and back to me. "How'd you know I'd need it to go?"

I look between her and Brett and try to hide my knowing smirk. I seem to have a knack for these things. "I wasn't positive, but I was pretty sure."

Brett rolls his eyes at me. "All right, you ready... I don't even know your name."

She looks up at him. "My name is Emma... Uh, I mean Heather."

Brett looks confused but nods his head. "All right, let's go grab your stuff. See you, Violet."

"Thanks, Violet," Heather says. Or Emma. I'm sure there's a story there.

Brett and Heather's story is out now.
Get Captivated now.
mybook.to/CaptivatedHopeFord

BONUS EPILOGUE
Want more of Austin and Millie's happily ever after? It's a good one. Keep reading

BONUS EPILOGUE

AUSTIN

Three Years Later

"Honey, I'm home," I holler as I walk into the house. There's chaos as I hear four little legs running full speed at me.

"Daddy, Daddy," the twins holler.

The dog, a one hundred thirty-pound black Labrador retriever, pounds after them and eventually passes them up. The dog gets to me first, but he's been trained not to jump, thankfully. He bounces all around me as the twins each grab on to a leg.

I lean down and pick them both up and settle them on my hips. "Hey, sweet girls."

They are identical and look exactly like their mother. I was nervous when I found out we were having girls. But Millie assured me it would be okay. So far, so good. However, I already have a plan to keep them grounded when they reach middle and high school. That's the only way I'm going to keep myself out of jail I think because I'm not going to be okay with any boy that's interested in dating my daughters.

They both bob up and down in my arms, excitedly trying to talk over each other. It's all a jumble as they go on and on about their day. They fed the chickens and gathered eggs. "We went and petted Patches," Mylie says.

And not to be outdone, Abby chimes in, "Yeah, and we played with the cats in the barn."

"Did Mommy ride Patches this morning?"

They both shake their heads. "No, she said she wasn't going to be riding her for awhile."

I try not to jolt at what Abby just said. That's not like Millie. She rides Patches every morning. That is one of her favorite things to do.

When I've nodded and hugged and kissed them until they want down, I ask, "Where is your mom?"

"She's up in the bedroom. We were making cookies with Carrie in the kitchen. Carrie said Pop Pop is coming for dinner."

I still can't believe it. Rusty, Millie's dad, came over for dinner one night after we got engaged and he and Carrie hit it off. What we thought would be a friendship turned into a wedding not even a year later. Carrie may have moved to the Ogles' ranch, but she's still here every day to help out. I was worried at first what Millie would think about it all, but after seeing how happy her dad is, there's no mistaking how much she loves having someone to be there for him. Plus, Millie and Carrie have gotten really close, giving the girls a grandma that spoils them.

"Okay, go save me a cookie and I'm going to go talk to Mommy."

They both run back to the kitchen, and I take the stairs two at a time, in a hurry to see my wife. It's been four years since I met Millie. Three and a half years since she said I do, and I swear I fall more in love with her every day.

I get to the closed bedroom door and push it open. My wife picks her head up off the pillow and sits up quickly. She pats the bed in front of her. I'm trying not to freak out, but I know it's coming. I know exactly what she's going to say, and I'm going to be sick.

I come to the side of the bed and sit down next to her.

"You okay, baby?"

She nods her head, her eyes not quite meeting mine.

"I missed you today."

She laughs then. "You came in for lunch."

I rub my hand up and down her leg. "The girls

said you didn't ride Patches today. You feeling all right?"

It's like everything stops. She takes a deep breath, and we're in a gridlock staring at each other. She's nervous, and I hate that. I don't ever want her to be nervous to tell me something, but I also know if she says what I think she's about to say, I'm going to lose it.

"Yeah, I'm feeling fine," she mutters before looking away.

She leans back against the headboard, and I move my hand to rub her belly. She's staring at my hand, and with my other one, I brush the hair from her face. "Is there something you want to tell me?"

I hold my breath because I know it's coming. I thought her breasts felt heavier last week and again last night. I knew she'd been tired more. I saw all the signs, but I chose to ignore them instead of asking her about them.

"Austin, I don't want you upset."

Finally, her eyes meet mine.

"You're pregnant," I accuse her. "We said we were going to wait."

She stubbornly lifts her chin. "Yeah, well, it takes two…"

"I know, Millie. I'm not blaming you, but I also can't watch you go through that again."

Where she was mad a second ago, she softens instantly. "I'm going to be fine."

"You could barely walk, you were in pain constantly… I just can't watch you go through that again."

She shakes her head. "Austin, it was pelvic girdle pain. It's not a death sentence. It's a little pain… and look at what we got for it. Two beautiful girls."

"I wouldn't trade the girls for anything, but you know it was more than just a little pain."

"Yeah, and the doctor said we can catch it early this time if I do have it again. I've been doing the exercises to strengthen my pelvic muscles. We're going to be ready this time."

"How did this even happen? I thought we were being careful."

"I think it was that night two months ago when the girls went and stayed at Dad's."

I think back to that night, and I remember it like it was yesterday. I let my foreman take care of the ranch for a straight twenty-four hours. We sent the girls to their grandparents' house, and I kept Millie in bed almost the whole time. I meant to be careful, but I know there were a couple of times that I forgot to take precautions.

Lost in thought, I don't notice that Millie is about to cry until a tear rolls down her cheek. "Honey, don't cry."

"I want you to be happy about this, Austin. We

made this," she says, rubbing her belly. "This little guy is a part of us. He needs us."

I put my hands on each side of her cheek. "I am happy about this. I'm scared, and I hate for you to be in pain. I'm going to take care of everything. You're going to lie around the house and stay off your feet, and Carrie will take care of the girls..."

"Austin..." she says, shaking her head.

"No, this is how it's going down, Millie. I need you. More than anything in this world, I need you. I won't be able to go on living without you, and I need to take care of you."

I wait for her to argue and disagree with me. She stares back at me for the longest time before she finally nods her head. "Okay."

"Okay? You mean you'll stay off your feet?"

"I mean I'll do whatever the doctor tells me I need to do." She pats my chest. "You know I love you just as much, Austin. That's why I'm so excited about this. I know it's a boy... I just know it. We're going to have a son."

Millie
Eight Months Later

"I told you so."

We're at the hospital, and I'm watching my husband as he stares in awe at the little bundle in his arms. "You told me what?"

"I told you that I was going to give you a boy."

Austin just smirks at me. "You can rub it in all you want, I'm not complaining."

Jacob Austin Yates was born less than three hours ago, and already Dad and Carrie brought in the girls to meet their little brother. They have been so excited to meet him, and I have no doubt they're going to be very helpful. Jacob just stared at them wide-eyed as they talked and cooed over him. He's so little now, but there's no doubt in my mind that one day he's going to tower over the both of them and protect his big sisters. Especially if he's anything like his daddy.

Violet also came to see the new addition to our family, and it's only now that I've been alone with Jacob for any amount of time. This pregnancy was so much easier than the twins' birth. And even though I had some pain, it was nothing like when I was carrying the girls.

Austin walks over to the side of the bed. He secures Jacob in one arm and touches my shoulder with his free hand. "You okay, Momma?"

"Come here." I have so many emotions inside me. I'm nervous about raising a boy. I don't know a lot about little boys, but Austin has promised he'll help me.

He leans over and cups my cheek. "What is it? You need something?"

My voice wobbles a little. "You. I need you, Austin Yates."

He looks into my eyes, and I swear the man gets me. He's always doing things for me. All I have to do is say the word, and he gives me what I want or need. Sometimes he even knows what I need before I know what it is.

He pulls the bassinet-type bed closer to us and lays Jacob in it. He's swaddled so tightly he doesn't even notice that he's no longer in someone's arms. We watch him sleep and relish in the fact that we did this… he's our miracle.

When Austin turns to me, his eyes have a fresh sheen of tears. He gathers me into his arms. "You have me, Millie. You will always have me. Thank you for giving me this life. You and the girls and now our son, you're my everything. I love you, baby."

I sigh against his chest. "I love you, too."

FREE BOOKS

Want FREE BOOKS?
Go to www.authorhopeford.com/freebies

JOIN ME!

JOIN MY NEWSLETTER & READERS GROUP

www.AuthorHopeFord.com/Subscribe

JOIN MY READERS GROUP ON FACEBOOK

www.FB.com/groups/hopeford

ABOUT THE AUTHOR

USA Today Bestselling Author Hope Ford writes short, steamy, sweet romances. She loves tattooed, alpha men, instant love stories, and ALWAYS happily ever afters. She has over 100 books and they are all available on Amazon.

To find me on Pinterest, Instagram, Facebook, Goodreads, and more:

www.AuthorHopeFord.com/follow-me

Printed in Great Britain
by Amazon

25773279R00067